The ROCKET Book

by
PETER NEWELL

CHARLES E. TUTTLE CO.: PUBLISHERS
RUTLAND, VERMONT

Published by the Charles E. Tuttle Company, Inc.
of Rutland, Vermont & Tokyo, Japan
with editorial offices at Suido 1-chome, 2-6
Bunkyo-ku, Tokyo, Japan

Library of Congress Catalog Card No. 69-12080
International Standard Book No. 0-8048-0505-9

First Tuttle edition, 1969
Sixth printing, 1990

PRINTED IN JAPAN

PETER NEWELL
(1862–1924)

An Appreciation

"No, the main reason that children of today cannot enjoy Peter Newell as we once did is that, for the moment, his books are not to be found. Thus he has reached exactly the spot in the cycle of celebrity that deserves rediscovery; for his books have been accorded the highest honor that children can bestow upon them; they have been thumbed right out of existence. Now they must be reprinted for the benefit of the children of today."

So wrote Philip Hofer, the distinguished authority on graphic art, in his charming 1934 *Colophon* article about the books of Peter Newell. Professor Hofer was a trifle premature in his prediction of a Newell Revival, for another thirty years had to elapse before our generation finally "discovered" the droll and engaging humor of one of America's most popular turn-of-the-century artists. With but a few exceptions, most of the books Newell wrote and illustrated are safely back in print, and in fact we have taken Professor Hofer's command so seriously to heart that *The Rocket Book* is his second work we have reprinted in less than two years.

Why is the work of Peter Newell so popular today? There is always, of course, the element of nostalgia on the part of older readers for the books of their childhood. Of more importance, perhaps, is the recent tremendous interest in 19th-century American art—an interest fortunately which has not neglected book illustration. The period in which Newell worked is now regarded as "the golden age of book and magazine illustration." One only has to mention such names as A. B. Frost, Frederic Remington, Howard Pyle, Dan Beard, N. C. Wyeth and even Winslow Homer. Such men made, as E. P. Richardson reminds us in his recent history of American painting, an important contribution to the development of objective realism through their close and penetrating observation of American life. One can find mirrored in the humor of Peter Newell a reflection of his early 20th-century America—the perils of urban living, as well as child and adult fads and interests of the time.

Of far greater importance in any re-evaluation of Newell is the great imagination and originality which give such zest and freshness to his work. When his intimate friend John Kendrick Bangs was asked to do an introduction for *Pictures & Rhymes,* he sought in vain for "influences" on the artistic career of Peter Newell. Although this particular book was similar in concept and execution to the *Nonsense Books* of Edward Lear, Newell never had read or seen these great English classics.

Such independence was typical of the artist who early decided that the value of his work lay in its originality. Impatient of academic training, he left the Art Student's League in 1882 after only three months of study. Professor Hofer also notes, for instance, that Newell developed his flat-tone technique in water-color painting quite unaware of the contemporary work of Maurice Bontet de Mouvel in France. Despite the perennial popularity of Sir John Tenniel's illustrations for *Alice in Wonderland,* Newell dared to interpret Carroll's classic for a new edition, which caused as much controversy then as the 1967 British television production starring Sir John Gielgud. Because of the uproar, Newell decided to defend his work in an article in the October, 1901 issue of *Harper's Weekly Magazine,* where he claimed that his intensely personal visualization of Alice justified his new interpretation.

This insistence on his own artistic freedom and integrity resulted in a style which was wonderfully spontaneous and varied—one which ranged from the quaint whimsy of "Wild Flowers" in *Pictures & Rhymes* (1899):

>"Of what are you afraid my child."
>inquired the kindly teacher.
>"Oh Sir, the flowers they are wild."
>replied the timid creature.

to the slapstick situation humor of *The Hole Book* (*c.* 1908), *The Slant Book* (*c.* 1910), and *The Rocket Book* (*c.* 1912). E. P. Richardson saw in Newell's fantastic humor "the first American appearance of the gentle humor of the absurd which *The New Yorker* has subsequently developed to such a high point."

However, Peter Newell was impatient with any formal analysis of his work; if he were to read the above, he no doubt would ask us to read the "New Year Anecdote" from *Pictures & Rhymes:*

> From Fox's *Book of Martyrs,*
> Aunt Matilda slowly read.
> "O aunt, turn over a new leaf,"
> her youthful nephew said.

So, lest this be wearisome, let us now indeed turn over a new leaf, and take a peek at Fritz, "the janitor's bad kid," who is about to light a rocket destined to have some amazing results. This book was originally published in 1912 by Harper & Brothers, New York.

THE ROCKET BOOK

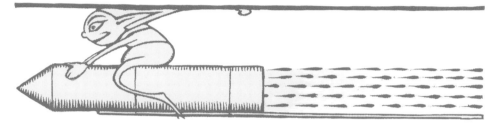

THE BASEMENT

When Fritz, the Janitor's bad kid,
   Went snooping in the basement,
He found a rocket snugly hid
   Beneath the window casement.

He struck a match with one fell swoop;
   Then, on the concrete kneeling,
He lit the rocket and—she—oop!
   It shot up through the ceiling.

FIRST FLAT

The Steiners on the floor above
  Of breakfast were partaking;
Crash! came the rocket, unannounced,
  And set them all a-quaking!

It smote a catsup bottle, fair,
  And bang! the thing exploded!
And now these people all declare
  That catsup flask was loaded.

SECOND FLAT

Before the fire old Grandpa Hopp
  Dozed in his arm-chair big,
When from a trunk the rocket burst
  And carried off his wig!

It passed so near his ancient head
  He roused up with a start,
And, turning to his grandsons, said,
  " You fellows think you're smart!"

THIRD FLAT

Algernon Bracket, somewhat rash,
  Had blown a monster bubble,
When, oh! there came a blinding flash,
  Precipitating trouble!

But Algy turned in mild disgust,
  And called to Mama Bracket,
" Say, did you hear that bubble bu'st?
  It made an awful racket!"

FOURTH FLAT

Jo Budd, who'd bought a potted plant,
  Was dousing it with water.
He fancied this would make it grow,
  And Joseph loved to potter.

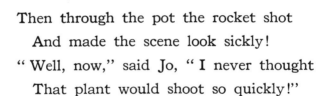

Then through the pot the rocket shot
  And made the scene look sickly!
" Well, now," said Jo, " I never thought
  That plant would shoot so quickly!"

FIFTH FLAT

Right here 'tis needful to remark
　　That Dick and " Little Son "
Were playing with a Noah's ark
　　And having loads of fun,

When all at once that rocket, stout,
　　Up through the ark came blazing!
The animals were tossed about
　　And did some stunts amazing.

SIXTH FLAT

A Burglar on the next floor up
  The sideboard was exploring.
(The family, with the brindled pup,
  Were still asleep and snoring.)

Just then, up through the silverware
  The rocket thundered, flaring!
The Burglar got a dreadful scare;
  Then out the door went tearing.

SEVENTH FLAT

Miss Mamie Briggs with no mean skill
  Was playing " Casey's Fling "
To please her cousin, Amos Gill,
  Who liked that sort of thing,

When suddenly the rocket, hot,
  The old piano jumbled!
It stopped that rag-time like a shot,
  Then through the ceiling rumbled.

EIGHTH FLAT

Up through the next floor on its way
   That rocket, dread, went tearing
Where Winkle stood in bath-robe, gay,
   A tepid bath preparing.

The tub it punctured like a shot
   And made a mighty splashing.
The man was rooted to the spot;
   Then out the door went dashing.

NINTH FLAT

Bob Brooks was puffing very hard
  His football to inflate,
While round him stood his faithful guard,
  And they could hardly wait.

Then came the rocket, fierce and bright,
  And through the football rumbled.
" You've got a pair of lungs, all right!"
  His staring playmates grumbled.

TENTH FLAT

The family dog, with frenzied mien,
  Was chasing Fluff, the mouser,
When, poof! the rocket flashed between,
  And quite astonished Towzer.

Now, if this dog had wit enough
  The English tongue to torture,
He might have growled such silly stuff
  As, " Whew! that cat's a scorcher!"

ELEVENTH FLAT

While Carrie Cook sat with a book
  The phonograph played sweetly.
Then came the rocket and it smashed
  That instrument completely.

Fair Carrie promptly turned her head,
  Attracted by the roar.
" Dear me, I never heard," she said,
  " That record played before!"

TWELFTH FLAT

De Vere was searching for a match
  To light a cigarette,
But failed to find one with despatch,
  Which threw him in a pet.

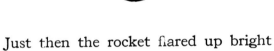

Just then the rocket flared up bright
  Before his face and crackled,
Supplying him the needed light—
  " Thanks, awfully," he cackled.

THIRTEENTH FLAT

Home from the shop came Maud's new hat—
　A hat of monstrous size!
It almost filled the tiny flat
　Before her ravished eyes.

When, sch-u-u! up through the box so proud
　The rocket flared and spluttered.
" I said that hat was all too loud!"
　Her peevish husband muttered.

FOURTEENTH FLAT

Tom's pap had helped him start his train,
  And all would have been fine
Had not the rocket, raising Cain,
  Blocked traffic on the line.

It blew the engine into scrap,
  As in a fit of passion.
" Who would have thought that toy," said pap,
  " Would blow up in such fashion!"

FIFTEENTH FLAT

Orlando Pease, quite at his ease,
  The " Morning Star " was reading.
" My dear," said he to Mrs. Pease,
  " Here's a report worth heeding."

The rocket then in wanton sport
  Flashed through the printed pages.
The lady gasped, " A wild report!"
  Then swooned by easy stages.

SIXTEENTH FLAT

Doc Danby was a stupid guy,
  So, lest he sleep too late,
He placed a tattoo clock near by
  To waken him at eight.

But, ah! the rocket smote that clock
  And smashed its way clean through it!
" You have a fine alarm," said Doc,
  " But, say, you overdo it!"

SEVENTEENTH FLAT

A penny-liner, Abram Stout,
    Was writing a description.
" The flame shot up," he pounded out—
    Then threw a mild conniption.

For through his Flemington there shied
    A rocket, hot and mystic.
" I didn't mean to be," he cried,
    " So deuced realistic!"

EIGHTEENTH FLAT

Gus Gummer long had set his head
  Upon some strange invention.
" Be careful, Gus," his good wife said;
  " It might explode. I mention—"

Just then the pesky rocket flared
  And wrecked that Yankee notion.
" I feared as much!" his wife declared;
  Then fainted from emotion.

NINETEENTH FLAT

While Burt was on his hobby-horse
  And riding it like mad,
The rocket on its fiery course
  Upset the startled lad.

The frightened pony plunged a lot,
  Like Fury playing tag.
" Whoa, Spot!" said Burt. " Who would have
    thought
  You such a fiery nag!"

TWENTIETH FLAT

A taxidermist plied his trade
   Upon a walrus' head.
It really made him quite afraid
   To meet its stare so dread.

●

When suddenly the rocket, bright,
   Flared up and then was off!
" Oh, Minnie," cried the man in fright,
   " Just hear that walrus cough!"

TOP FLAT

Oh, it was just a splendid flight—
  That rocket's wild career!
But to an end it came, all right,
  As you shall straightway hear.

It plunged into a can of cream
  That Billy Bunk was freezing,
And froze quite stiff, as it would seem,
  And so subsided, wheezing.